This book belongs to:

_____

_____

_____

To my son, Ryan,

who LOVES to build rock piles and paint with his dinosaur.

NEVER LET A DINOSAUR SCRIBBLE!

Written & Illustrated by
Diane Alber

I recently got a pet dinosaur. I know it's hard to believe, but it's true. And everyone keeps telling me **NEVER LET A DINOSAUR SCRIBBLE!**

Why would anyone say such a thing?
I mean, dinosaurs are so strong and powerful!
So why can't they scribble?

I thought if I gave him just ONE crayon,

what could go wrong?

Well...I'll tell ya...

He took off running towards the wall!
"WE DON'T SCRIBBLE ON WALLS! ONLY PAPER!" I yelled.

Thank goodness my dinosaur has a short attention span. Just before he was going to scribble on the wall, he noticed a couple of stones instead...

He started to scribble on one of the stones!
Which was great!

But there was just one
problem...

He really couldn't see the scribble at all...

I could tell he had another idea...

HE WENT TO GRAB THE PAINT!

This wasn't going to end well.

But surprisingly, it didn't make as big of a mess as I thought.
He just quietly painted his little stone, and it turned
out awesome!

But then he got ANOTHER idea...

He wanted to paint

DINOSAUR-SIZED STONES!

It didn't take long before he was rolling boulders
into the room, one after another!

It had become the biggest rock pile

I HAD EVER SEEN!

And the way he painted the rocks was truly extraordinary! But you couldn't see my floor or my bed anymore! I had to find a place for this rock pile, and quick!

Then I heard a noise down the hall...

This was it! I was going to be in so much trouble!
I popped my head out of the door.
My mom was standing right there.
Before my mom could say anything, I started
to explain the mess she was about to see...

"Well, it all started when I heard to never let a dinosaur scribble.

But I had to find out why.

So I gave my dinosaur a crayon, and then he ran towards the wall with it!

Thank goodness he got distracted with some small stones and started scribbling on them instead, but he couldn't see the scribble at all, so he got some paint!

He loved it so much that he got bigger stones, giant ones even and it made a big mess...and...I'm sorry."

My mom peeked around the corner and smiled, "You didn't make a mess! You made some spectacular stone ART!"

When I turned around, there was just a little pile of stones on my table. No huge boulders and no gigantic rock pile.
But still some of the best art ever!

All this time people wanted to stop dinosaurs from scribbling. It could be because they try and draw on walls. Or make a gigantic rock pile. But if my dinosaur had never scribbled, he would have never learned how to make this amazing stone art! So the next time you hear NEVER LET A DINOSAUR SCRIBBLE just remember...

All great art starts with a scribble...
and even dinosaurs have to start somewhere!

The End.

Made in the USA
Las Vegas, NV
29 January 2023